To Ruisaurie

A Walk with Grannie
by Mairi Hedderwick
British Library Cataloguing in Publication Data
A catalogue record of this book is available from the British Library.

ISBN 0 340 86642 x

Text and illustrations copyright © Mairi Hedderwick 2003

2 4 6 8 10 9 7 5 3 1

First published 2003
by Hodder Children's Books,
a division of Hodder Headline Limited,
338 Euston Road, London, NW1 3BH

Printed in Hong Kong

A Walk With Grannie

Mairi Hedderwick

Hodder
Children's
Books

A division of Hodder Headline Limited

Bye bye,
Daddy and Beedee dog
and peckiedoos.

Kirsty is going
for a walk with
Grannie.

Hi-ya, Ashie,
   here is your carrot.

Hi-ya, Gregor and Bob.

Bob is behaving so well
in Gregor's beautiful garden.

Hi-ya, bath.

How strange,
   a bath in the grass.

Hi-ya, gloomy house.

Anyone there?

Hi-ya, pheasant.

Where are you going?

Hi-ya, Mrs MacKay.

The wind is good for the washing.

Hi-ya, bull moos,
sheltering in the shed.

Hi-ya, home!

But look, it's not home,
it's the farmer's house.
Time to turn round.

Bye bye, farmer's dog,
and peckiedoos.

Bull moos are out of their shed.
Look at their earrings!

Bye bye,
bull moos.

Tup baas have disappeared.
Where to?

Bye bye, tup baas.

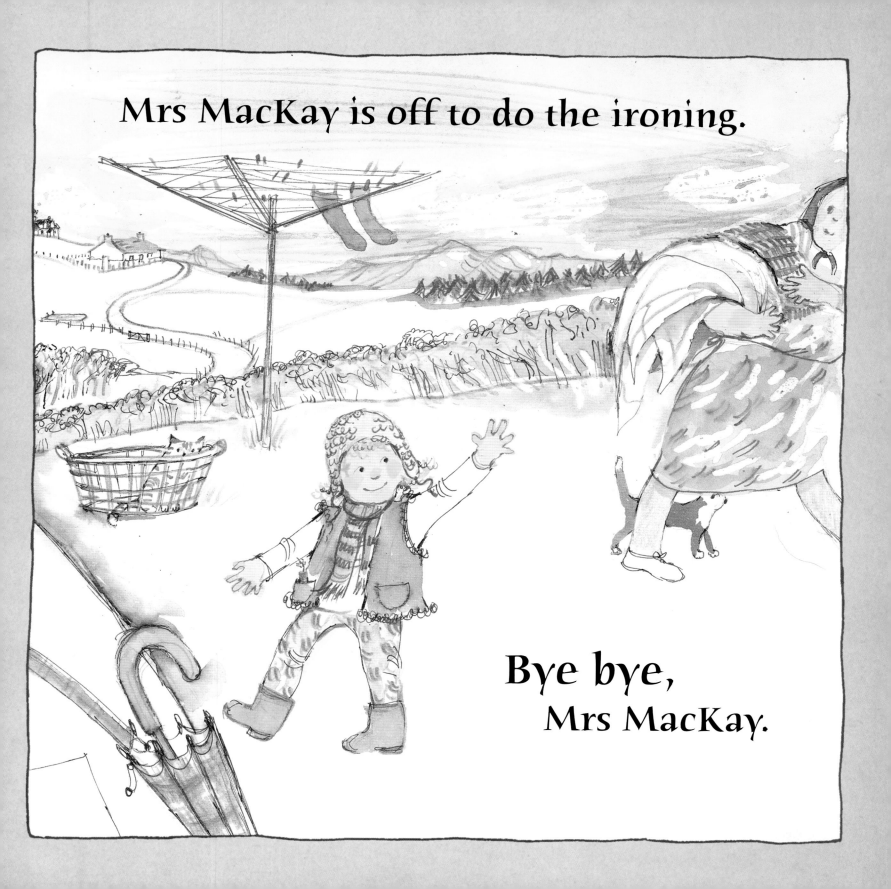

Mrs MacKay is off to do the ironing.

Bye bye,
Mrs MacKay.

Pheasant is gone. Where to?

Bye bye,
pheasant.

Gloomy house is still there.
Is that **someone** at the window?

Bye bye,
gloomy
house.

A bath in the grass. What a good idea!

Bye bye,
bath.

Nearly home. Here are some flowers for Mummy and Daddy.

Oh dear!

There are pheasant
and tup baas
and Bob –
behaving
badly.

And Ashie;
no carrot for you!

Bye bye, Gregor.
Oh dear!

Hi-ya, Beedee dog and peckiedoos.
Hi-ya, Daddy, hi-ya, MUMMY

and hi-ya, new baby Erika!

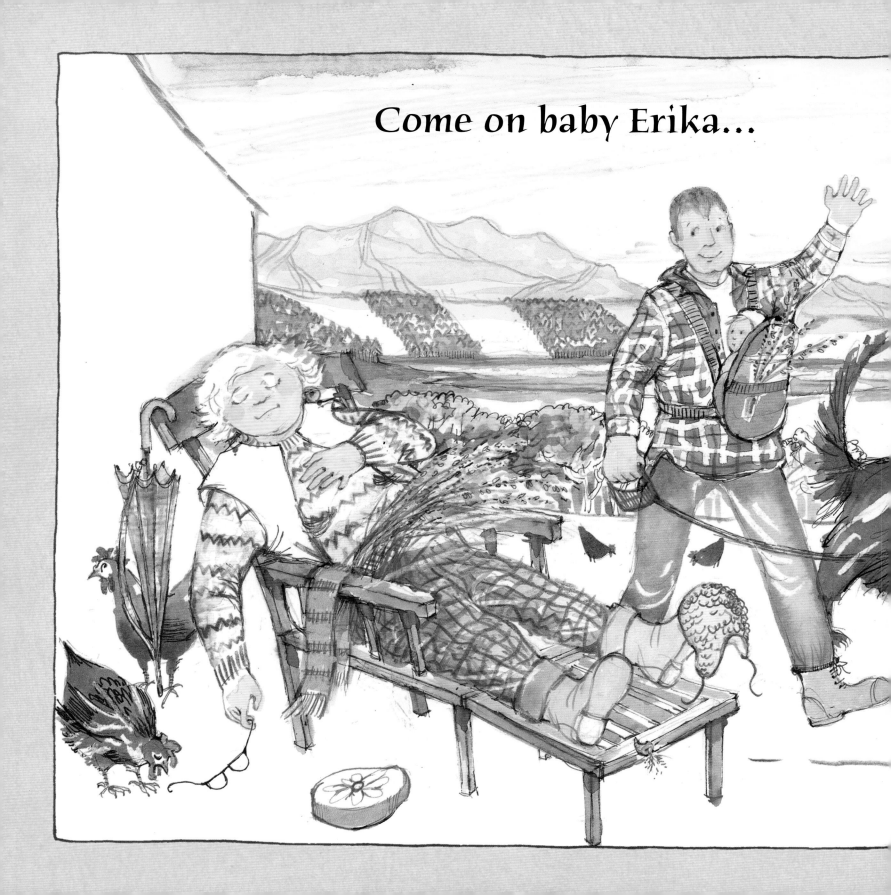

Come on baby Erika…

Let's say hi-ya to the tup baas
and the bull moos and Bob...

Bye bye,
Grannie!